HE Robot Inventor's Handbook

ROBOTIX

BUILD THE ADVENTURE

Printed in Hong Kong.

9 8 7 6 5 4 3 2 1
Digit on the right indicates the number of this printing

Library of Congress Cataloging-in-Publication Number 99-75086

ISBN 0–7624–0741–7

Photo research by Susan Oyama
Cover and interior design by Bill Jones
Assembly diagrams courtesy of Learning Curve International, Inc.
Edited by Jason Rekulak
Typography: Helvetica Condensed and Officina Serif Bold

The kit containing this book may be ordered by mail from the publisher. Please include $2.50 for postage and handling.
But try your bookstore first!

Running Press Book Publishers
125 South Twenty-second Street
Philadelphia, Pennsylvania 19103-4399

Visit us on the web!
www.runningpress.com

THE Robot Inventor's Handbook

BY GREGORY VOGT AND DEBORAH SHEARER

RUNNING PRESS
PHILADELPHIA • LONDON

Table of Contents

Chapter One
The Robots Are Coming!

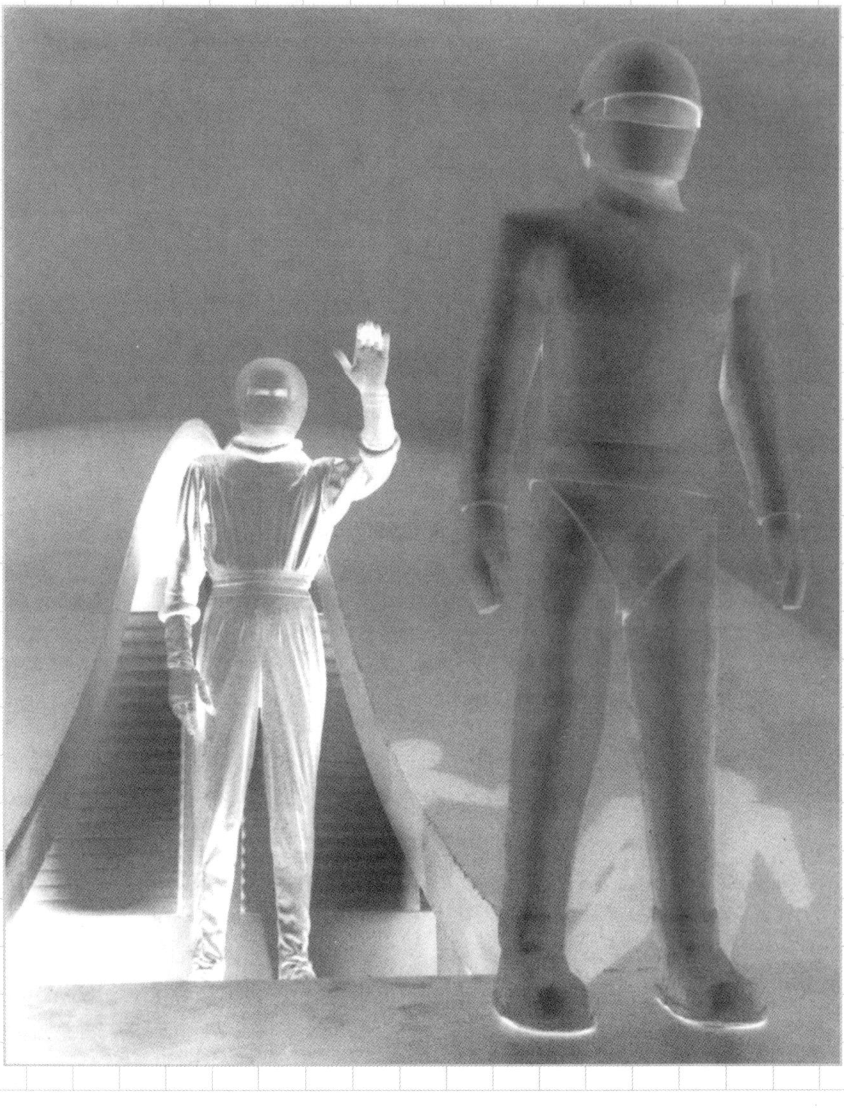

"We have come to visit you in peace and with good will."

The Martian Klatu spoke to the thousands of spectators and soldiers surrounding the flying saucer. The spacecraft had landed on the grassy mall of Washington, D.C. after circling the world at the incredible speed of 4,000 miles per hour. Klatu, dressed in a spacesuit with a bulbous helmet, stepped onto the grass and approached the soldiers. As he got closer, he reached inside his spacesuit and removed a gift for the President of the United States. A nervous soldier, believing the gift was a weapon, panicked and shot Klatu, striking him in the shoulder.

As Klatu slumped to the ground, a second Martian visitor emerged from the spaceship. This Martian was an 8-foot-tall humanoid robot. Terrified spectators ran away in a stampede but the soldiers held their ground. A visor opened on the robot's face. His eyes cast a laser-like beam of light at the nearest soldiers. Their rifles glowed brightly and disintegrated! Then the robot set his eyes on a tank—it glowed brightly and dissolved into a glob of molten metal! The robot would have continued the destruction but Klatu called for him to stop.

(Previous page) Klatu and the robot Gort from the movie, *The Day The Earth Stood Still.*

"Gort!" Klatu yelled. "Iglasio Crosko!"

Gort turned off the beam and the visor dropped back into place.

Back in 1951, when the movie *The Day The Earth Stood Still* introduced Gort, most people only knew robots from science fiction movies.These robots were shaped like humans. They had the strength of a thousand men. And they almost always went haywire!

Today, most people think they know a robot when they see one—but do they really?

Which of these things are robots?

- **Mechanical arms that assemble automobiles in factories**
- **Home VCRs**
- **Traffic lights**
- **Automatic dishwashers**
- **Elevators**
- **Home air conditioning and heating units**
- **Clock radios**
- **The Mars Sojourner**
- **Supermarket scanners**
- **Automatic Teller Machines**
- **Automobile cruise controls**

Believe it or not, the answer is all of the above. You may not think of these devices as robots, but they are. In fact, you probably have dozens of interactions with robots every day.

Which may prompt you to ask: Just what are robots, anyway? Where did they come from? How do they work? What do they do? And most importantly: Can you build a robot? The answer to that last question is "Yes!" The parts that come with this book will enable you to construct a working robotic arm, plus other robot inventions limited only by your imagination.

What Is a Robot?

Every dictionary has its own definition of a robot. The Robot Institute of America offers this one:

A robot is "a programmable, multifunctional manipulator designed to move material, parts, tools, or specialized devices through various programmed motions for the performance of a variety of tasks."

Huh?

Let's simplify that. Robots are:

- **machines with moving parts that do jobs in place of humans**
- **controlled by a computer brain**
- **programmable**

That's better! Now, let's see how that applies to some of the robots we mentioned earlier.

Automatic Teller Machine (ATM): A person approaches the machine and inserts a plastic identification card. The computer screen asks for a personal identification number. After the number is entered, the computer asks the person how it can help. By punching the right buttons, the person says, "Give me $100." The ATM accesses the account, deducts $100 from the total, and pushes the bills through a slot. Over the past few years, these "robot bankers" have replaced many human tellers.

Home Air Conditioner/Heater: Mom or Dad programs the thermostat with a desired temperature. A special climate-sensing device determines when the house gets too hot or cold. This device turns on the air conditioner or heater to adjust the temperature of the house. The robot works all day even if Mom or Dad are away.

Elevator: A passenger waiting for an elevator will push the UP button. A computer determines which elevator car is nearest to the passenger's floor and heading in the right direction. The car is sent to the floor and the doors open automatically. The passenger steps on, and another push of a button sends the car to the desired floor.

Each of these robots makes our lives easier. The thermostat saves us the trouble of stoking the furnace. The ATM enables the bank to be open twenty-four hours without human tellers being present.

The elevator saves us the time and effort of climbing stairs. By performing these tasks, robots free us to do more important or enjoyable tasks.

Where Do Robots Come From?

To answer this question, we must travel 2,800 years back into history. The idea of robots existed long before people had the capability of building them. According to an 8th century B.C. Greek legend, women were made from gold and brought to life to help Hephaestus, the god of fire, do his work. In the 1st century B.C., the ancient Greeks built a temple that contained what may have been the first working robotic device; at the end of the day, when a fire went out, this robot would close the temple doors automatically.

After people learned to build complex clockworks in the 16th and 17th centuries, many more robot devices were constructed. Inventors began to make fantastic toys and dolls that appeared to write, draw pictures, and play instruments.

In 1738, the French inventor Jacques de Vaucanson invented a mechanical copper duck that could eat, drink, make noises, and produce duck droppings. We're not kidding—it actually left behind a trail of robotic duck poop. Yeecchhhh!

Soon, inventors realized the technology in these toys could be put to practical use. They strove to create machines that were stronger and faster than human labor. These devices could make cloth, grind wheat, print books, package beverages and food, and manufacture automobiles. Today, we would call these devices "robots," but the word didn't come into being until after the 1920s.

Fictional Robots

The word "robot" was first used in a play written in 1920 by Czech playwright Karel Capek. The play was called *R.U.R*, which stood for *Rossum's Universal Robots.* Robot came from the Czech word "robota," which means forced labor. Capek's play described what would happen if robots were invented to take over human labor. Eventually (as would happen in many science fiction movies) the robots got smart and decided they no longer needed their human creators. You can imagine what the robots did.

Another important fictional work on robots was the book *I, Robot*, written in 1950 by Isaac Asimov. Asimov formulated three laws of robotics that all advanced robots had to obey. The laws are:

- **A robot may not injure a human being or, through inaction, allow a human being to come to harm.**

- **A robot must obey orders given by human beings except where such orders would conflict with the First Law.**
- **A robot must protect its own existence as long as such protection does not conflict with the First or Second Law.**

Asimov's laws influenced the behavior of many fictional robots that appear in movies and television shows. You can probably name dozens of these—like best friends C3PO and R2D2 (of the *Star Wars* movies), Rosie the housekeeper (from the TV show *The Jetsons*), and the android Data (from the TV show *Star Trek, The Next Generation*). But these kinds of robots exist only in movies and television. So you might be wondering: What do robots in *our* world look like?

Real Robots

The kinds of robots we know today got their start in the 1950s. The first industrial robots were created to do heavy or boring jobs on factory assembly lines. These robots had powerful arms that could lift auto body frames and place them on conveyor belts. Other factory robots can weld metal, put labels on bottles, print newspapers, and bind books.

(Below) These assembly line robots are welding a truck.

In recent years, even more sophisticated robots have been introduced. Computer factories use miniature robotic arms to handle tiny microchips. The FBI uses "bomb-sniffing" robots to find explosive devices and diffuse them. There are even robot "doctors" in hospitals that perform precise surgical procedures. All of these might seem hard to believe—but they are just a few of the possibilities. In the next chapter, we'll look at the most common applications for today's robots.

A "bomb-sniffing" robot searches a suspect car in Belfast, Northern Ireland. No bomb was found.

Chapter Two
The Three Ds

Robots are perfect for doing jobs that are classified as the "Three Ds." The Ds stand for **dull, dirty, and dangerous.** Robots don't mind jobs that are boring and repetitive. They can work in an environment full of smelly fumes, and they're not afraid of doing a job that could injure or destroy them.

Booorrriiinnnggg!

Imagine having a job in a factory where you take three new tennis balls from a bin and slip them in a plastic tube. You do this job for 8 hours a day, day after day, week after week. The job would get pretty boring. Soon you would begin to make mistakes. This kind of job would be perfect for a robot to do. Robots never get bored and never make mistakes.

Robots are great for assembling small parts, putting labels on bottles, folding and gluing boxes, and packing products. It might seem like robots are stealing all the jobs from human beings, but this isn't exactly true. Robots only take jobs that are dull and repetitive, and they generate many more interesting jobs in robot maintenance, engineering, and design.

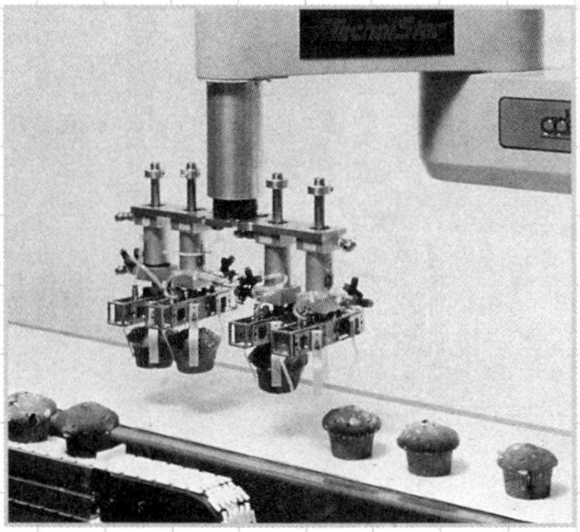

Slime, Grime, and Other Dirty Stuff

In the movies, robots appear shiny, polished, and new. In real life, robots are usually very dirty—but they don't mind. Some robots dig through garbage moving on conveyor

(left) This robot lifts and packs muffins at the Otis Spunkmeyer factory.

(opposite) Dante II robot is "brave" enough to explore active volcanos.

belts to find recyclable materials. The smell must be terrible—but robots never complain! Robots also handle chemicals, mold products from plastic, and print newspapers and magazines. Each of these jobs can produce toxic fumes, but robots never get sick (and never ask for worker's compensation).

Danger, Will Robinson!

Robots can perform risky jobs that might cause a human to be hurt. When a nuclear power plant has an accident, the human operators must be very careful. Dangerous radiation could be leaking from the reactor. So the humans often send in a robot with a video camera and radiation detectors to inspect the equipment. If everything is fine, the humans can fix the problem without risk.

Offshore oil platforms are also dangerous places to work. Sometimes there are problems with the drilling equipment, which is deep beneath the ocean surface. A human being could never swim to such great depths—but a submersible robot could dive to the bottom with a video camera. An operator on a surface ship can assess and repair the problem with the robot's arm. (If you've seen the movie *Titanic*, you'll know that the shipwreck was explored with similar technology.)

(Above) When there are accidents at sea, a deep drone robot may be used to recover lost property.

(Right) This robot is designed to move and stack boxes.

Chapter Three
Robot Mechanics

If you're going to build robots, you need to become an expert in robotic mechanics. For all their varying designs and purposes, most robots share several things in common:

- **A body or base which contains the robot's control systems**
- **At least one arm that ends with a gripper, which is called an *end effector* (we'll explain why later)**
- **Wheels (if the robot is mobile)**
- **A power system that provides a lifeline of energy**
- **A sensory system that will help the robot "see" its environment**

Over the next two chapters, we'll discuss how robots use these features, and how you can choose from different options to design your own robots.

Robot Bodies

You may have seen robots at museums and festivals that "welcome" human tourists. These robots walk, twirl, flash lights, shake hands, spin their heads, and carry on conversations. Pretty cool, right?
Yet most people never notice that one "tourist" is really not a tourist at all—this person is the robot's operator! A book or a purse hides the radio transmitter unit that controls the robot. You may also see the operator pretend to drink from a beverage cup. But hidden inside that cup is a radio receiver and microphone that the operator uses to make the robot "talk."

The truth is, most real robots do not look like people, and they probably never will. Robot bodies are usually in the shape of boxes, cylinders, or spheres. But whatever the shape, it is always determined by a robot's function. A robot designed to inspect the inside of pipelines

for fractures must be small enough to fit inside a pipe. And a robot designed to move pallets of supplies in a warehouse must have a heavy body, like the base of a fork lift, to keep the robot from tipping over.

End Effectors

At the end of every robotic arm is what designers call an *end effector*. You might wonder, "Why not just call it a hand?" But the truth is, most robotic arms do more than just lift and move objects. The term *end effector* describes any device on a robotic arm that has an effect on its environment. For example, a robotic arm that paints automobiles would have a paint spray nozzle. And an arm that assembles computer chips might feature a tiny soldering iron.

(Right) Dante II has explored the world's most dangerous volcanos.

(Below) These robots use their end effectors to paint cars.

Here are a few more examples of end effectors:

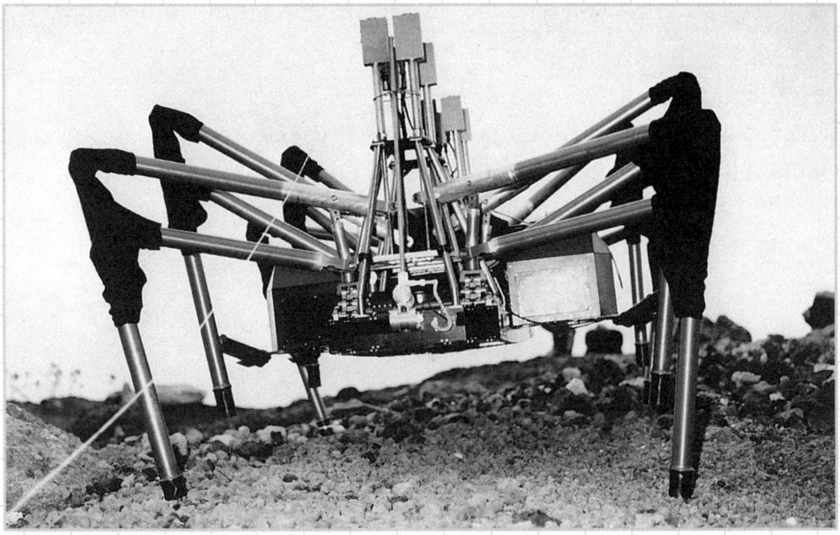

Recycling Robot—Every day, in recycling plants around the country, millions of aluminum soda cans are processed along conveyor belts. It is important that stray steel cans are removed from the mix. Rather than hire humans to sort through the cans, factories will use magnet end effectors to pluck out the steel cans (which are magnetic) from the aluminum cans (which are not).

Exploration Robot—Geologists would love to study the inside of an active volcano—but no human being would be crazy enough to go inside one! It's much safer to send a walking robot into the crater. The robot's end effector, working like a nose, inhales the air and stores it in a small tank. This air will be analyzed later in a chemistry laboratory for different gases given off during an eruption.

Planetary Spacecraft—Wouldn't you like to examine soil samples from Mars? Many scientists would, too, but it's very expensive to send astronauts into space.

It's much more affordable—and safer—to send a remote-controlled robot to our neighboring moons and planets. Using a small shovel end effector, the robot can dig a hole in the planet's surface and store the sediment for future analysis.

Wheels

Many years will pass before we design a robot that is capable of walking in any terrain. It

takes thousands of calculations just to design a robot that can "walk" on a flat, solid surface—but what happens when that robot encounters a flight of stairs? Or a patch of sand? Or a pool of water? As you can guess, most walking robots do a lot of tripping, shuffling, stumbling, and falling.

So if you want your robot to be mobile, stick with wheels. Many robots only need two wheels to get around—if these wheels both spin in the same direction, the robot can advance forward or go backwards. But if these wheels move in opposite directions at the same time, the robot will turn left or right. To keep the robot from falling over, a leg with a very smooth foot is placed beneath the robot to make a tripod base. As the robot moves, the leg slides across the floor. Many toy robots use this technique for getting around.

(Left) This six-wheel Mars rover was designed by Russian and American scientists.

More advanced mobile robots have four, six, or even eight wheels. The Sojourner robot sent by NASA to explore Mars had six wheels, so it could travel easily over rocky terrain. The extra wheels made sure that part of the robot was always touching the ground, so that Sojourner wouldn't get stuck.

Power to the Robots!

Robots are powered in a variety of ways, but the power source is usually determined by a robot's task. Most factory robots have an electric motor, so they are simply plugged into a wall socket. But if the robot has to move around, it requires an onboard power system. Batteries are easy to use, but they can be heavy. A mobile robot can use up much of its battery power just from carrying its battery weight One alternative is solar cells, which convert sunlight to electricity. These work very well, unless it's dark outside. Many robots are equipped with a combination of batteries and solar cells. Robots that need a lot of strength depend on hydraulic power. You have probably seen hydraulic lifts in automobile service stations. They work like this: Oil is pumped from reservoirs into cylinders. Extending from the center of the cylinders are pistons or rods that are pushed out by the pressure of the oil. The pistons slowly raise the automobile into the air, so that service technicians can stand under it and do their work.

A similar (but much smaller) lift cylinder is used to move the arms of a robot. The cylinder is located at the joints of the robot's arms. When oil is pumped into the cylinder, the piston extends and pushes the arm up. If the oil is pumped back to the reservoir, the piston sinks into the cylinder and this lowers the arm.

Pneumatic robots are similar to hydraulic robots, but the cylinders use air instead of oil. And since air is lighter than oil, pneumatic robots weigh less than hydraulic robots, and can move faster. On the downside, pneumatic arms aren't as strong as hydraulic arms, because air is compressible.

Degrees of Freedom

By now, you are nearly an expert in robot mechanics, but there is one more thing you should know. Designers like to describe a robot's capability in terms of "Degrees of Freedom." This is simply the number of different ways the robot can move.

(Right) Hydraulic lift

Let's start with an imaginary robot. The robot has wheels that enable it to go forward and back. That is one degree of freedom. But the wheels can also steer, which enables the robot to go left or right. That is a second degree of freedom. Our imaginary robot also has an arm that can rotate at the base and bend at the shoulder, elbow, and wrist. That adds four more degrees of freedom. Finally, the robot has a gripper end effector that can open and close—yet another degree of freedom. This robot has a total of seven degrees of freedom.

Congratulations! You are now an expert in robot mechanics!

(Right) This robot has a ring of 24 infrared and sonar sensors—which means it can "see" in 24 different directions.

Chapter Four

Sensing the Environment

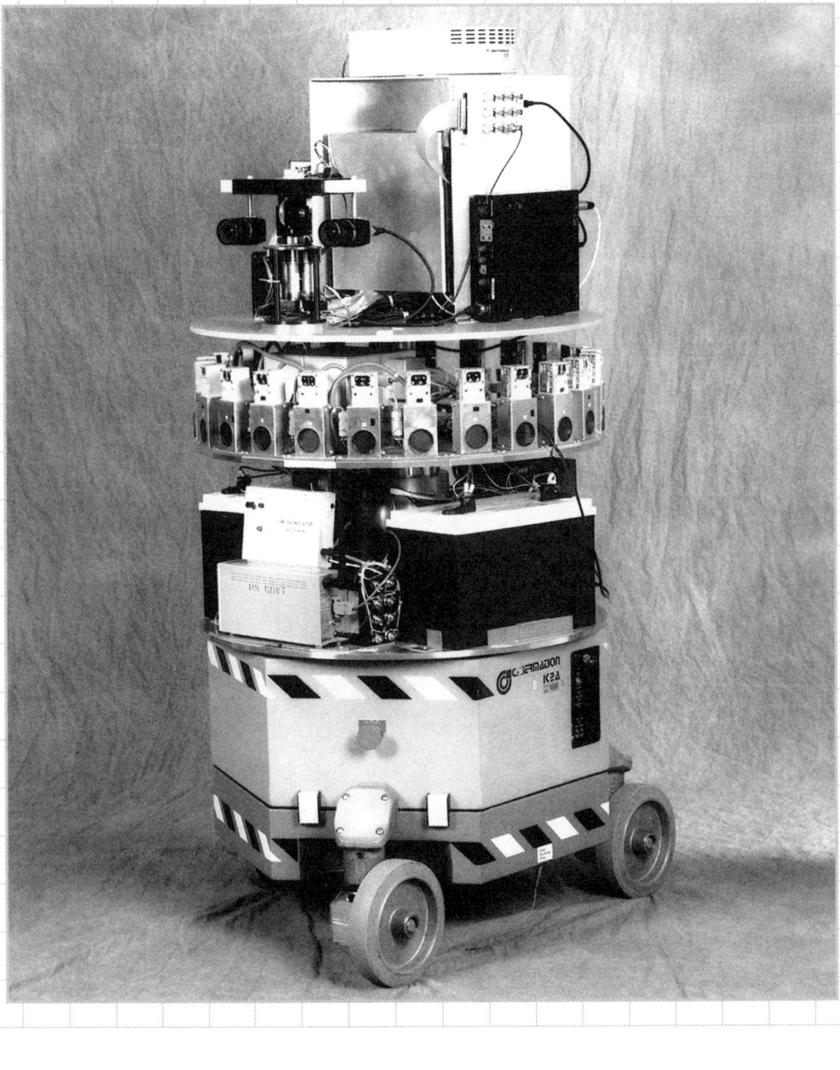

Most robots are like puppets. You sit back with a controller and tell the robot exactly what to do. If the robot has a video camera, you can watch its actions on a television screen and provide instruction by remote control. Robot designers call this method of operating a robot *telerobotic control.* This method of controlling robots is fine, but it doesn't save you much time. Wouldn't it be nice to have a robot that worked without supervision? Absolutely—but designing such a robot creates new challenges.

This Mars Pathfinder Rover can analyze rocks to determine their mineral composition—and send the information to scientists on Earth.

Operation: Mailbot

Pretend for a moment that you are a professional robot inventor, and you need to design a speedy "Mailbot" that would deliver letters throughout a large office building. You begin by selecting a robot with wheels and a computer control system. Then you equip the robot with pouches that will hold mail for the different offices. Finally, working with a map of the building, you program a computer to send "Mailbot" on a carefully planned route, designated with many stops to deliver and receive letters.

When it is time for Mailbot to start working, a human attendant fills up the pouches with mail. Then, the attendant pushes the GO button. Mailbot comes to life and heads out the automatic double doors. At its first stop, Mailbot toots a small whistle. A secretary steps into the hall, removes mail from the pouch, and places outgoing mail in a basket. Then the secretary taps the GO button and Mailbot is off to another stop.

Sounds like the perfect invention, right?

Maybe you'll even be voted Robot Inventor of the Year!

But after a few hours, something unexpected happens. A clumsy office worker spills some coffee in the hallway and leaves to get paper towels. Meanwhile, Mailbot is turning the corner and heading right for the spill. As Mailbot splashes through the puddle, its right wheel slips an inch. This makes Mailbot think it has made a turn, but it really hasn't. And so poor Mailbot rides through an open doorway, tumbles down a flight of stairs, and spills all of the mail. And you, the robot inventor, are out of a job.

But if Mailbot had been equipped with sensors, this wouldn't have happened.

Sensors

Sensors make observations about the environment. They tell the robot's control system where it is, which way it is heading, and how fast it is going there.

Sensors come in many forms. Some can be as simple as rubber bumpers with small switches. If a robot crashed into a wall, the bumper would trigger a switch, alerting the computer to an obstruction. The computer would stop the robot, adjust the direction, and try again. This process would be repeated until the robot eventually found an open doorway.

This kind of navigation is effective but slow-going. Smarter robots are equipped with light sensor systems. In this system, the sensor looks for a bright light and aims the robot toward it. If the room is dark and the doorway is bright, the robot has no trouble heading in the right direction. Another method is to aim the light sensor at the floor. If the floor is made of dark floor tiles with a white line running across it, the robot will follow the white line. Even if the line curves, the robot will follow it and head down the hall.

More advanced robots use electromagnetic currents to find their way. With this system, a series of electric wires must be placed under the floor tiles. When electricity flows through the wire, a small magnetic field is produced. Using magnetic sensors, a robot can sense the wire and follow it to each stop. So even if coffee is spilled on the floor, the robot can tell it is going astray and get back on course.

Extremely advanced robots depend on sonar systems. These robots send out low-pitched sounds that bounce off

(Right) This robot works in a Mississippi hospital. It can make rounds, move around obstacles, call for its own elevator, and move from floor to floor without the help of a human.

HelpMate

objects in the nearby vicinity. The robot records the length of time it takes for the sound to bounce back—and learns the location of all the nearby objects in its surroundings. The robot's computer will adjust the route so the robot can travel without hitting anything. This kind of sensor system is similar to how bats fly in the dark.

Robotic arms can also be equipped with sensors. If the arm is designed to pick up eggs, a pressure sensor will tell the robot when it has grasped an egg and how hard the gripper is squeezing.

Sensor systems are an important part of advanced robots. After all, what good is a robot if you always have to control it? With a good set of sensors and the right computer, you can program a robot to do anything—and you'll have plenty of time leftover to bike, read, play ball, or just hang out.

(Right) An artist's rendition of the Mars Surveyor Lander. A mobile rover will gather information from the surface of the planet, and the Lander base will transmit the data to scientists on Earth.

Chapter Five
Futurebots

Almost every kid dreams of a robot that would do his or her homework. But the fact is, you may already have a robot helping you. If you've ever typed a report on a computer, then you've probably asked a robot printer to "write" all of the text for you! Remember, there are already dozens of household robots, like VCRs and answering machines, in your day-to-day existence.

But the future will introduce robots that we can hardly imagine. Here's a sneak peek at some of the "futurebots" you are likely to encounter.

Transportation Robots

Robots are already used as autopilots in commercial airplanes, but soon cars will have autopiloting systems too. You'll program your car with a destination and a preferred arrival time. A navigation system will make all of the calculations and you'll be on your way. Instead of driving the car yourself, you can watch TV, read a book, or just look out the windows. The robot autopilot will steer the car, maintain safe speeds, avoid traffic jams, and never get into an accident.

Elevators will also take on new directions. They'll still move up and down, but they'll also move sideways, transporting you to the room or adjoining building of your choice. In the future, you won't just push floor buttons on the elevator. You will enter a specific room number into a key panel.

Around the House

When you spill some milk in your kitchen, you have to get out a mop and clean it up. But future household robots will do the work for you. A sensor grid on the kitchen floor will awaken the robot. About the size of a small dog, this robot will zip out to the spill and lap it up. Other robots will vacuum carpets, pick up toys, and prepare dinner. While you're away from home, security robots will keep an eye on your house, chase away intruders, and even put out fires. When you return home, your robots will turn on the lights, play some music, and bring you something to drink.

Police and Military Robots

Dealing with criminals and defending our nation will become a safer occupation with futurebots. Small robots the size of insects will fly around and scout out trouble with their surveillance systems. When something bad is happening, human police can arrive on the scene in moments. Violent criminals will be safely subdued with robots. Robots will dispose of bombs and other dangerous weapons. Robots will also be used to supervise jails. The miniature flying robots will be good for military operations. They will be able to locate the enemy without putting human scouts at risk. Other robots will be used for the dangerous job of clearing out mine fields.

Space Exploration

Robots will continue to be used to explore the solar system. Many of the planets are too dangerous for humans to get near. Jupiter is surrounded by intense radiation fields and Venus is extremely hot. Yet robots will explore these places. On planets like Mars, robots and people will work together to explore its surface and to construct permanent colonies.

One space futurebot is close to reality. The International Space Station will have a very long robotic arm that will move cargo and do repairs. The arm will ride on a cart along a long support beam to the location of its next job. If the cart cannot reach the next destination, the robot will grab on to a special fixture and let go of the cart. Then the arm will move freely around the station, crawling from fixture to fixture like a giant inchworm.

Robots of the future will serve us in many ways. But, in order for these robots to exist, people like you will have to design and construct them.

So what are you waiting for? Let's build robots!

Chapter Six
Let's Build Robots!

ROBOTIX®
BUILD THE ADVENTURE™

Your ROBOTIX Robot Inventor's Workshop

In this kit, you will find a motor, controller with a black cord that plugs into the motor, an assortment of arm pieces, three straight connectors, and two elbow connectors. Keep in mind that Robotix® components are very durable; even if you wiggle and squiggle the parts around, they will not break with regular use.

To get started, you need to put two AA batteries in the controller. Now plug the black cord into the motor, turn on the controller and watch for the moving gear. This is where you'll attach pieces that need to move. Now let's get started!

1 CONTROLLER WITH CORD

1 MOTOR

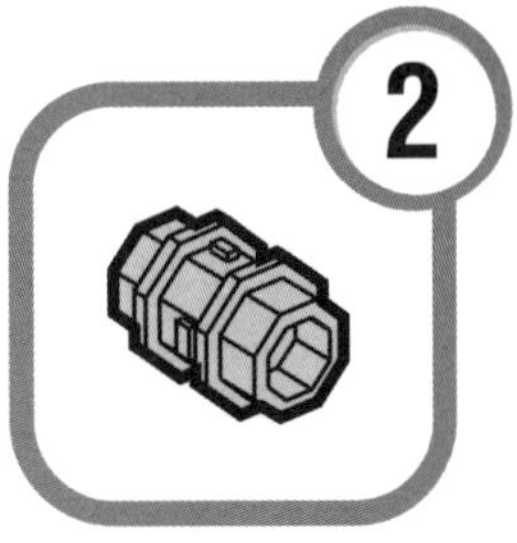

2 MALE/MALE CONNECTORS

2 ELBOW CONNECTORS

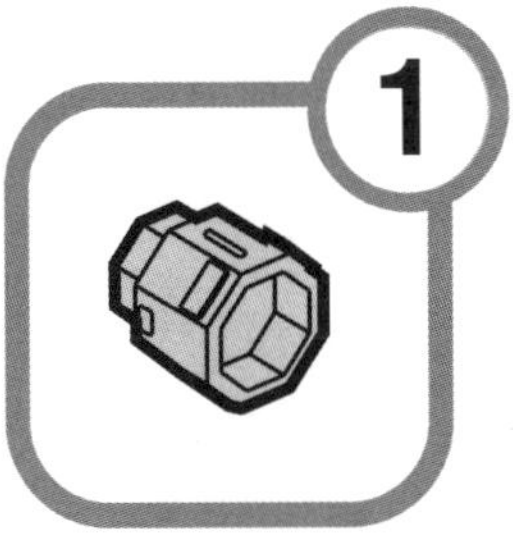

1 MALE/FEMALE CONNECTOR

10 SHORT ARMS

5 LONG ARMS

For replacement parts, or if parts are missing,
contact Robotix at 1-800-704-8697
or via e-mail: cs@learningcurve.com

Challenge One:
Create Your Own Robotic Arm

To build your arm, follow the simple steps diagrammed below.

1

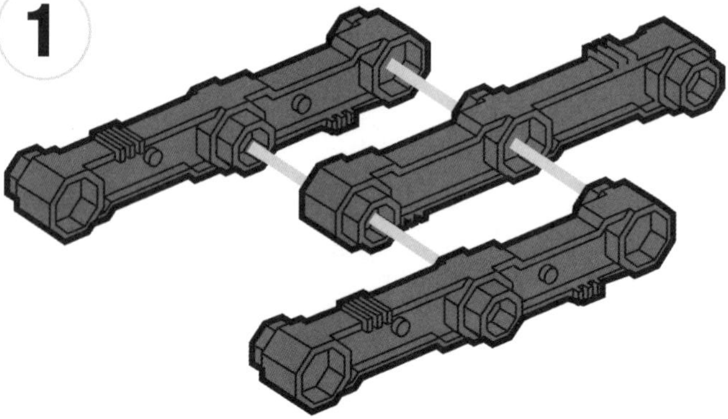

2

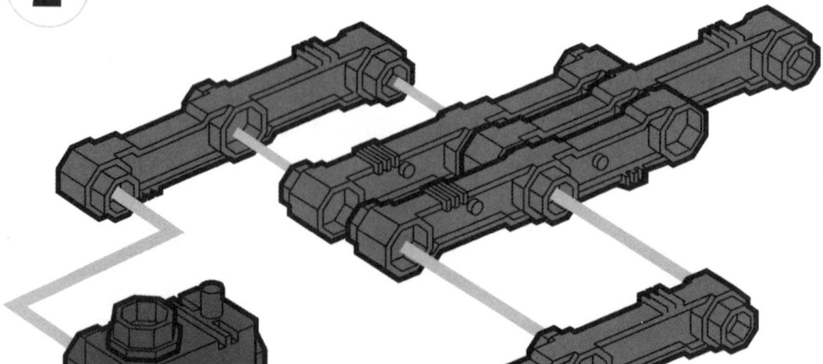

3

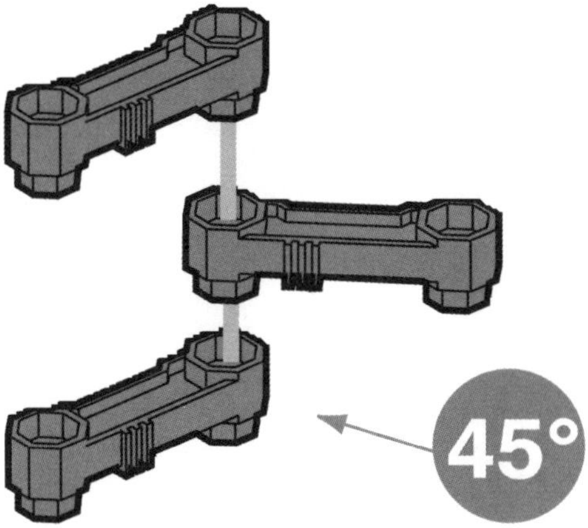

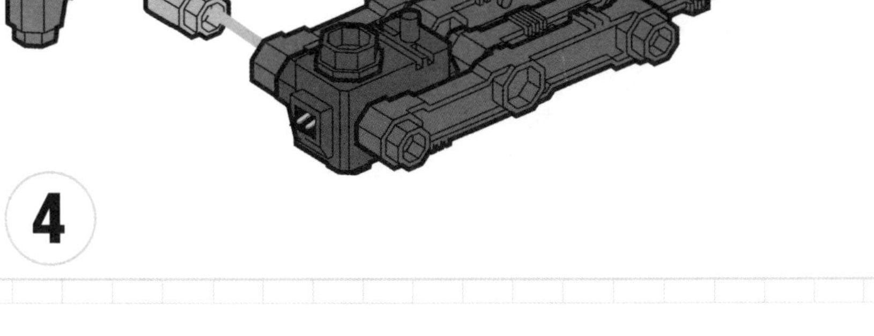

4

5

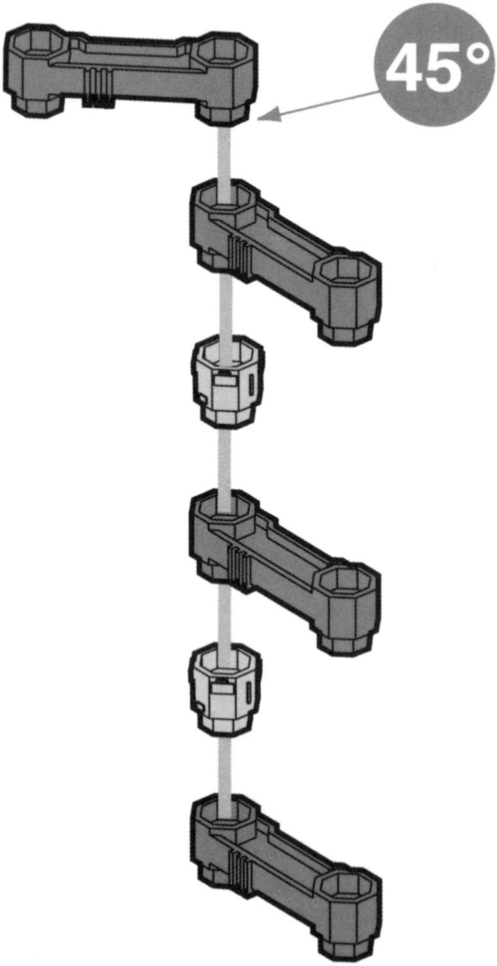

7

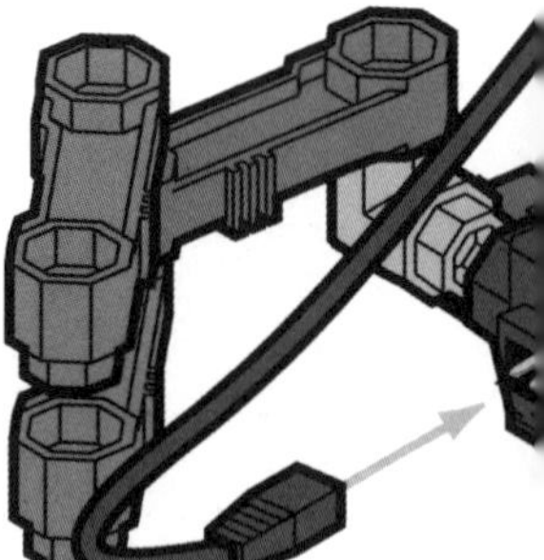

6

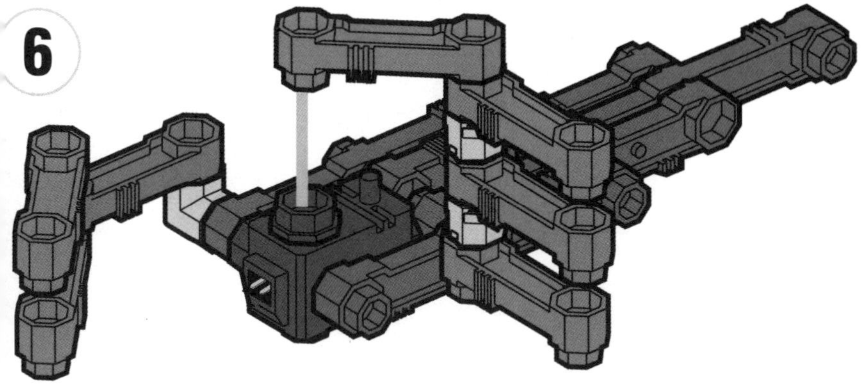

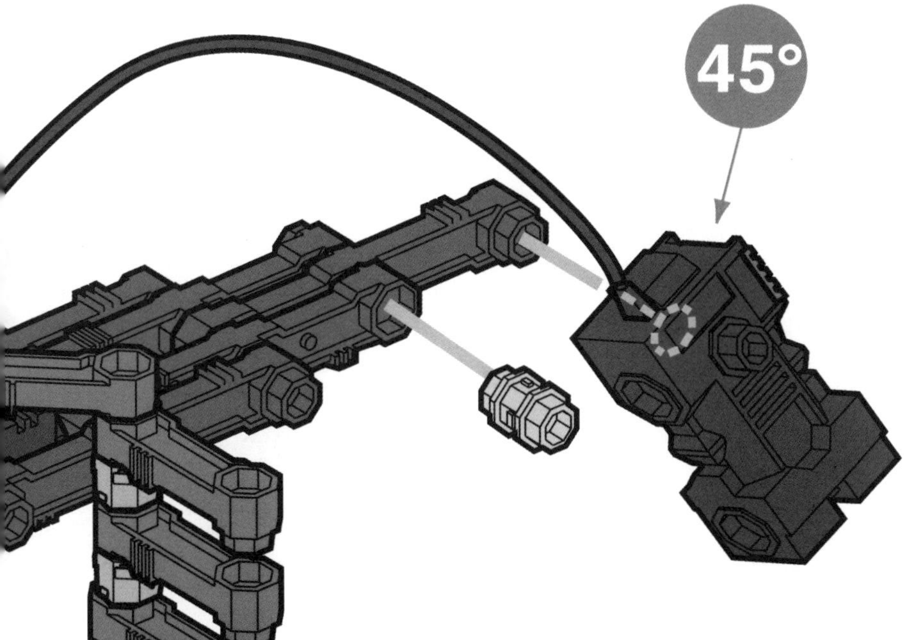

8

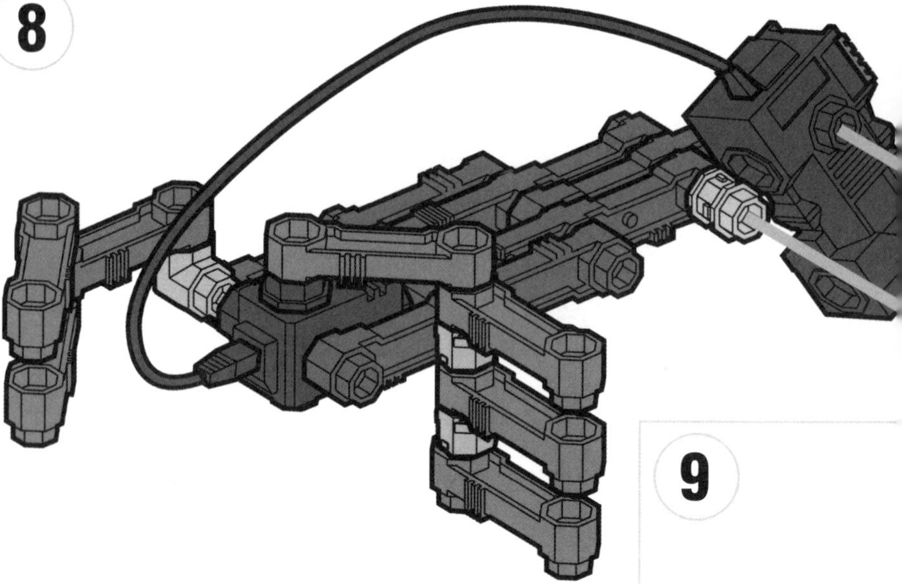

9

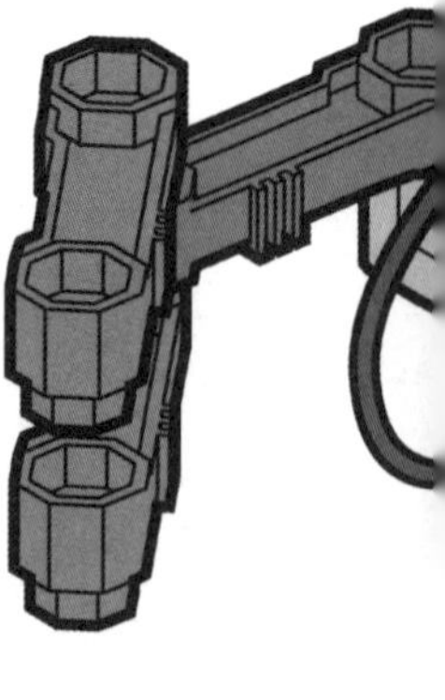

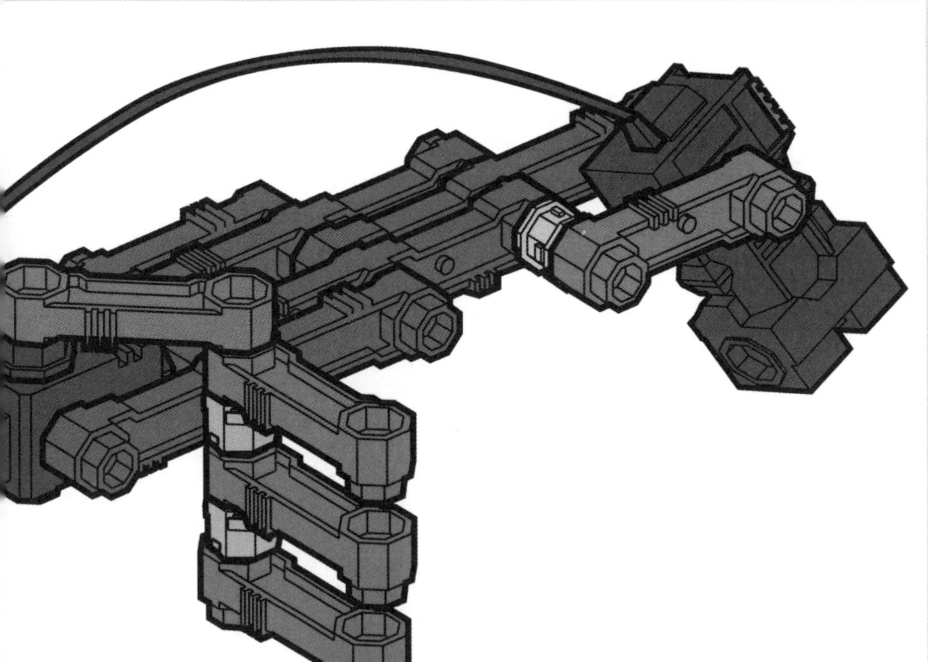

Challenge Two:
End Effector in Action

You already know that the robot arm has an end effector. This is a tool that has an effect on its environment. In this instance, it is a robotic hand with three fingers on one side and two on the other. But can your robotic hand perform these simple tasks?

What You'll Need:

- **empty soda can**
- **tennis ball (or other small ball)**
- **pencil**
- **egg (be careful here)**

Get started:

Place the objects on the edge of a table in a line. With your robotic arm, try to pick up each individual item, bring it to the end of the line, and put it down. Some of these objects will be more difficult than others. Which ones were the hardest for you? Why do you think so?

If you found an object that you could not pick up with the end effector, what can you do to complete the task? Hint: if your hand has trouble "getting a grip," try wrapping rubber bands around the fingers. This will add friction. Can you think of other solutions?

Challenge Three:
Build a Pulley Power Hoist

Scientists would love to extract unseen minerals and metals from the crust of the moon, and we've designed a robot that can perform the task—but it requires a very skillful human operator!

What You'll Need:

- **Five metal paper clips**
- **12-inch string, shoelace, or dental floss**

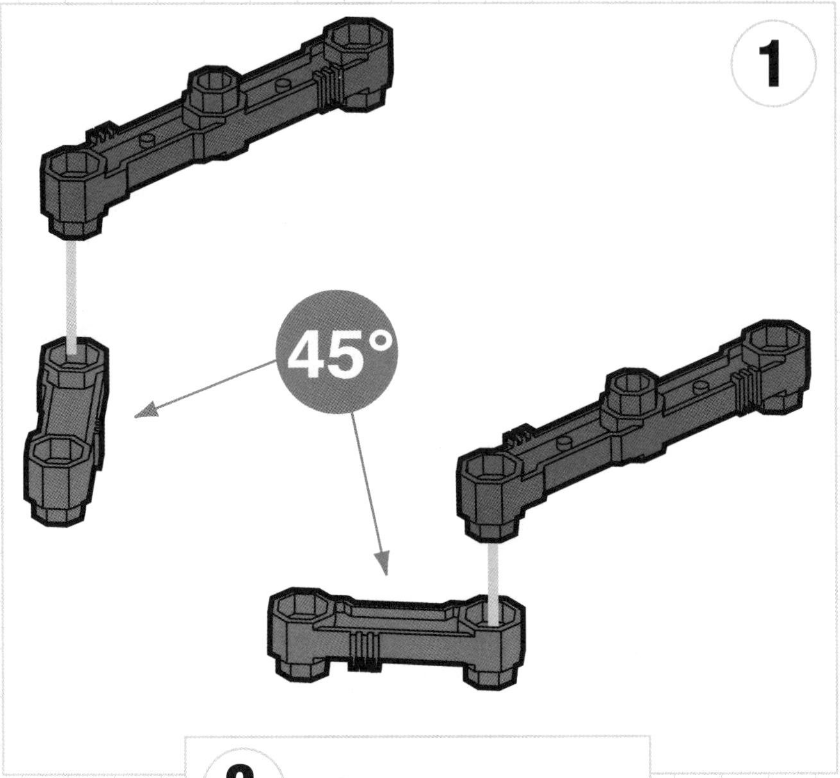
1
45°

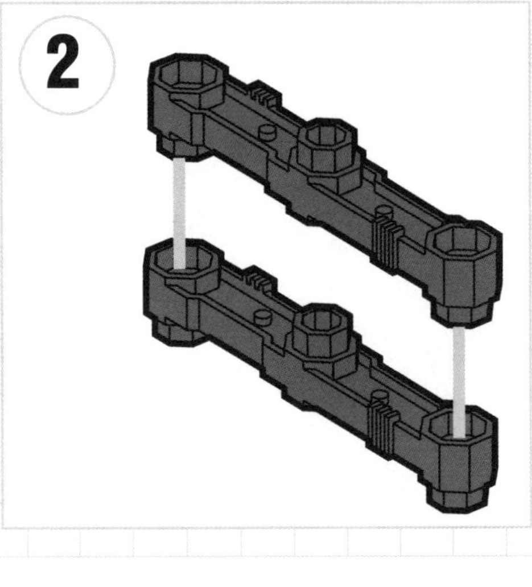
2

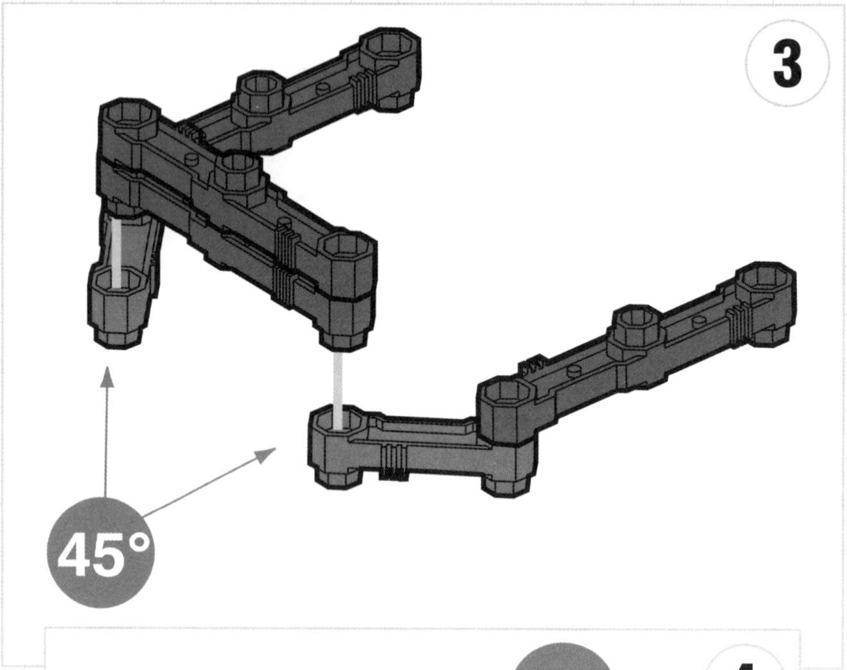
3
45°

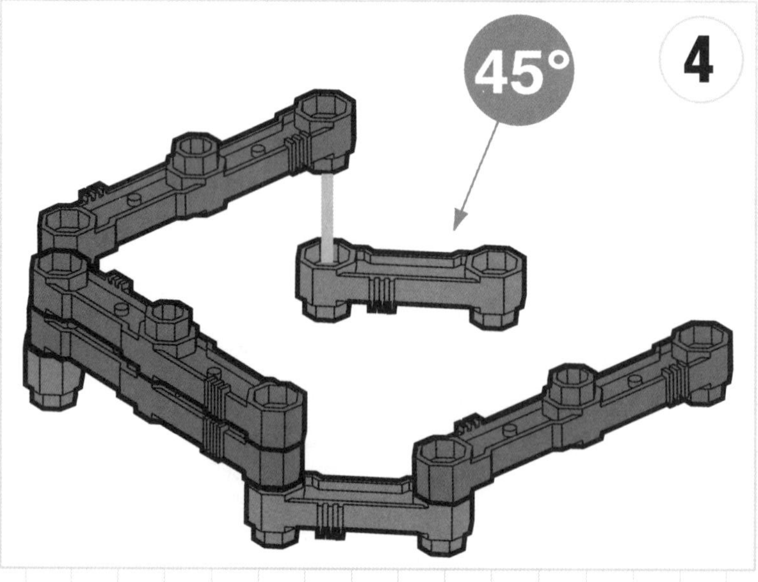
4
45°

5

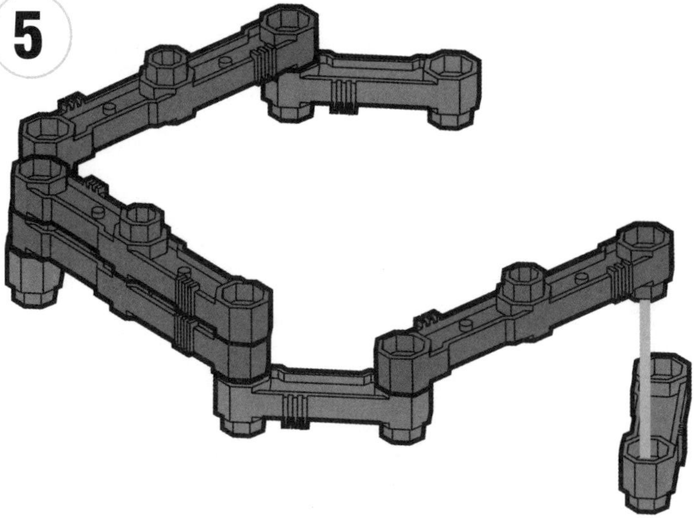

6

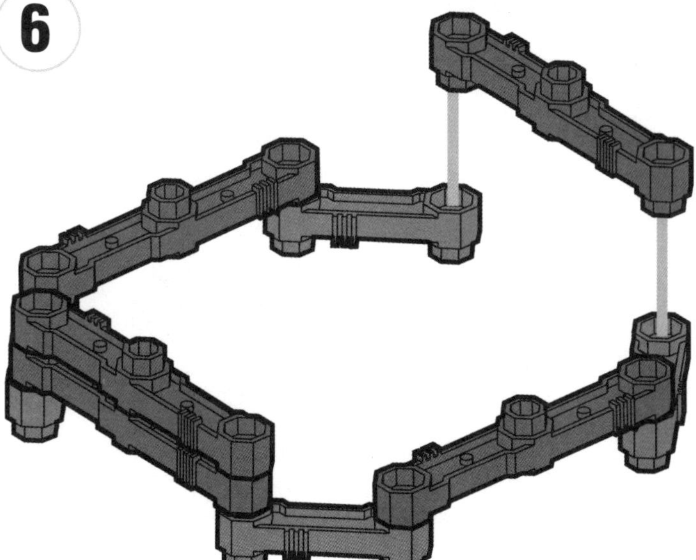

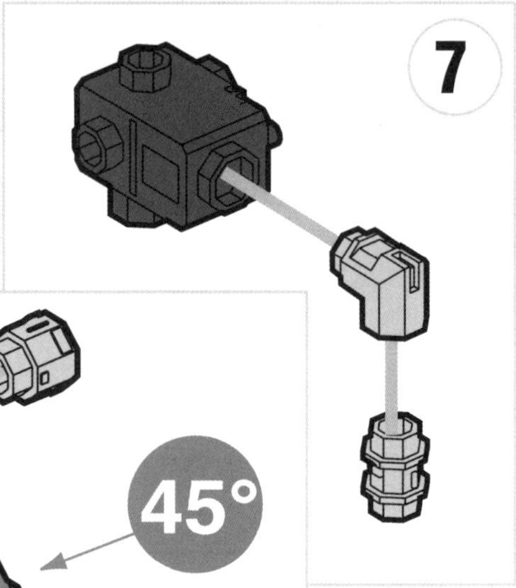
7

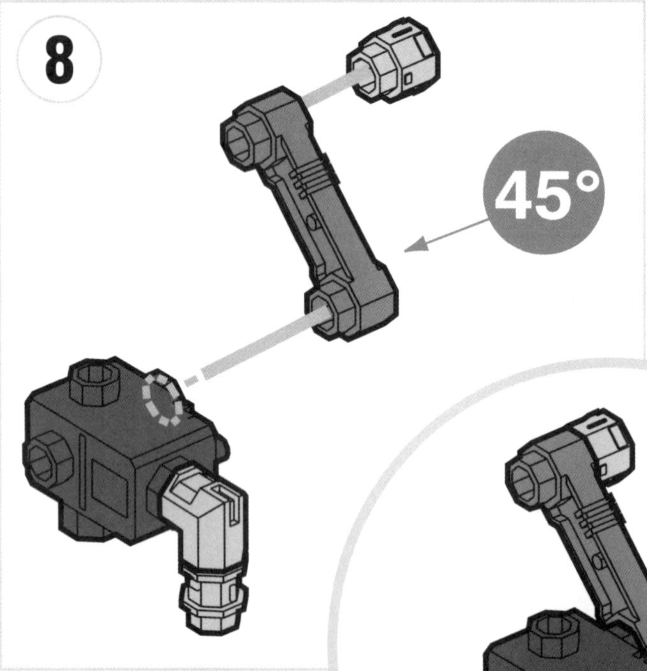
8
45°

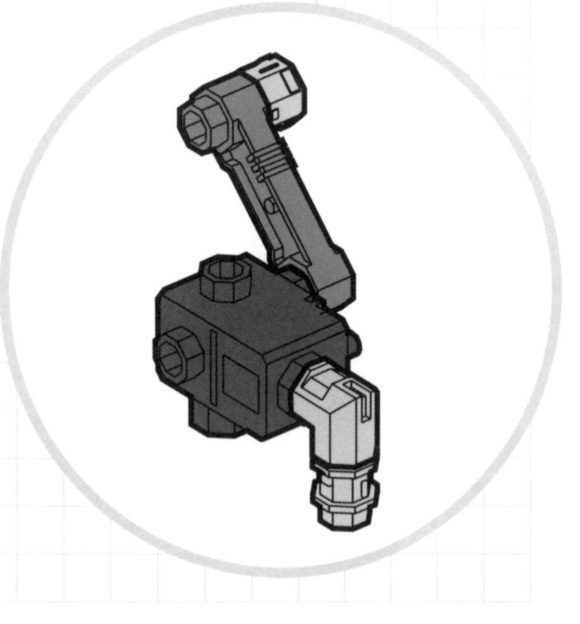

9

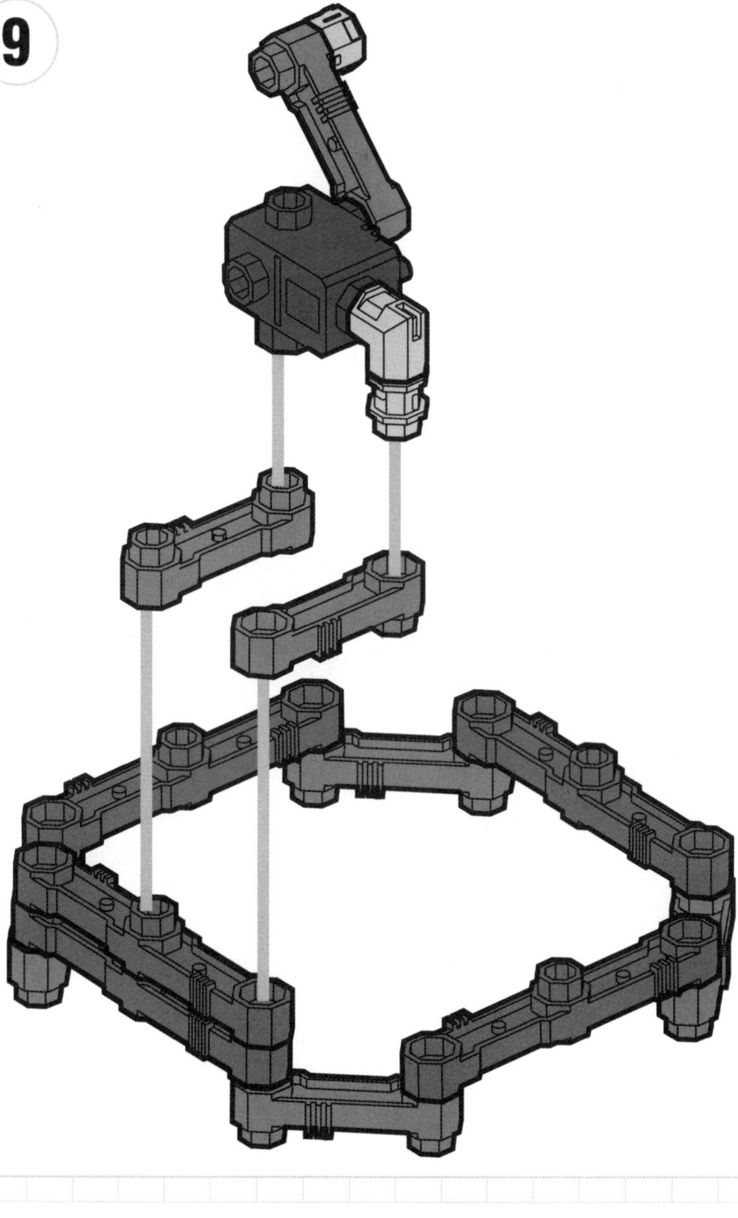

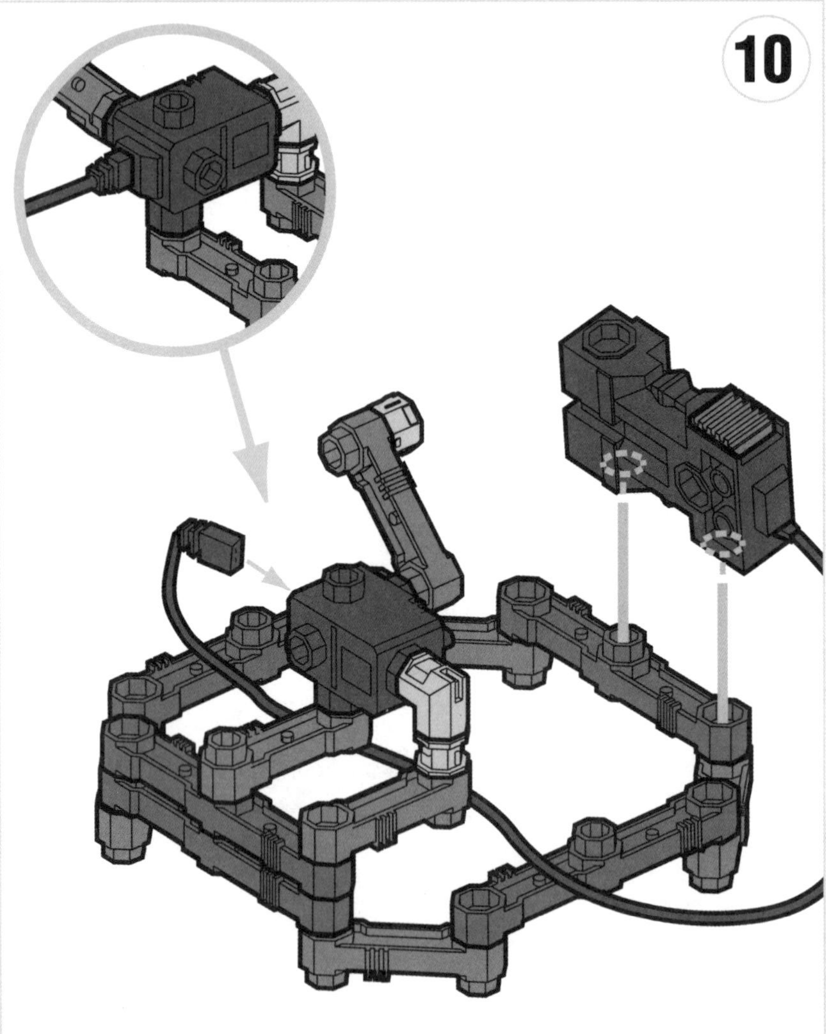
10

11

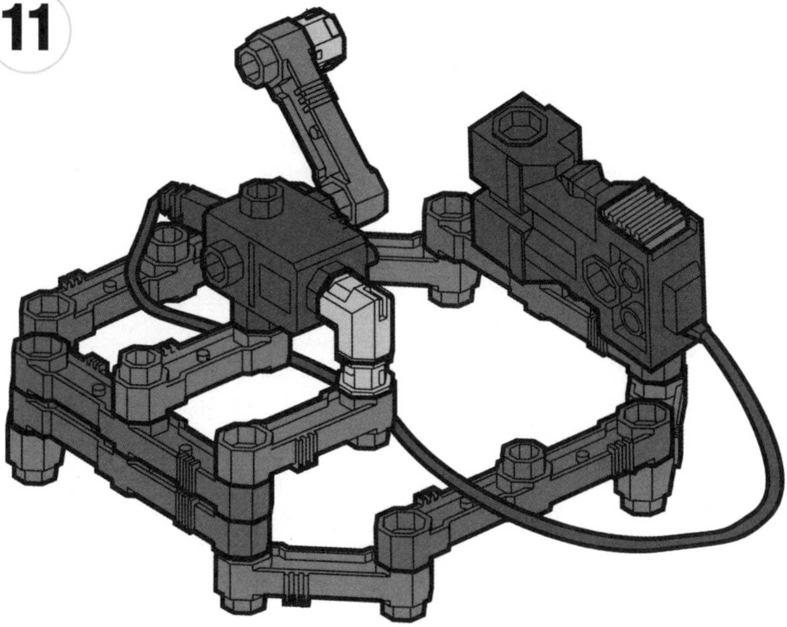

Get started:

Open four of the paper clips into bent "V" shapes. Then go into your backyard or sandbox and dig a narrow hole that's at least six inches deep. Place the Pulley Power Hoist over the hole. Take the four bent paper clips and drop them in the hole; these are the "precious metals" you need to retrieve. Make a hook out of the fifth paper clip and tie it to the string; tie the other end of the string to the "arm" on the motor. How many of the valuable metals can you retrieve?

Challenge Four:
Build a Lunar Crawler

What You'll Need
- **Rubber bands (optional)**

In this challenge, you'll build a Lunar Crawler that can creep over rocky terrain. If you use this robot on a carpet or smooth floor surface, try wrapping a few rubber bands around the moving feet; this friction will allow the robot to "plant" its feet and take stronger steps.

As an experiment, you can also trying adding rubber bands to the rear (stationary) feet. Adding friction to these feet will cause the robot to move more slowly, because you are increasing the resistance. For maximum performance, you'll want these feet to slide as smoothly as possible!

Below is a diagram of a crawler for you to build. However, the true challenge lies in developing a better and faster crawler to creep across the surface of the moon. Let's get started—see if you can beat us!

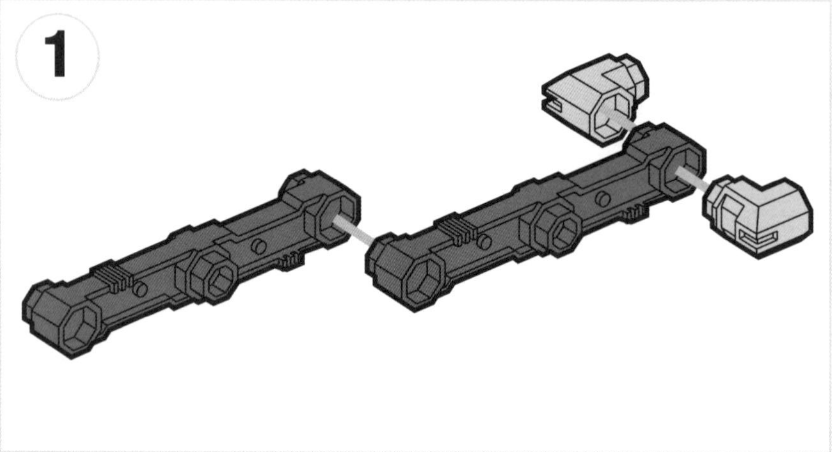

2

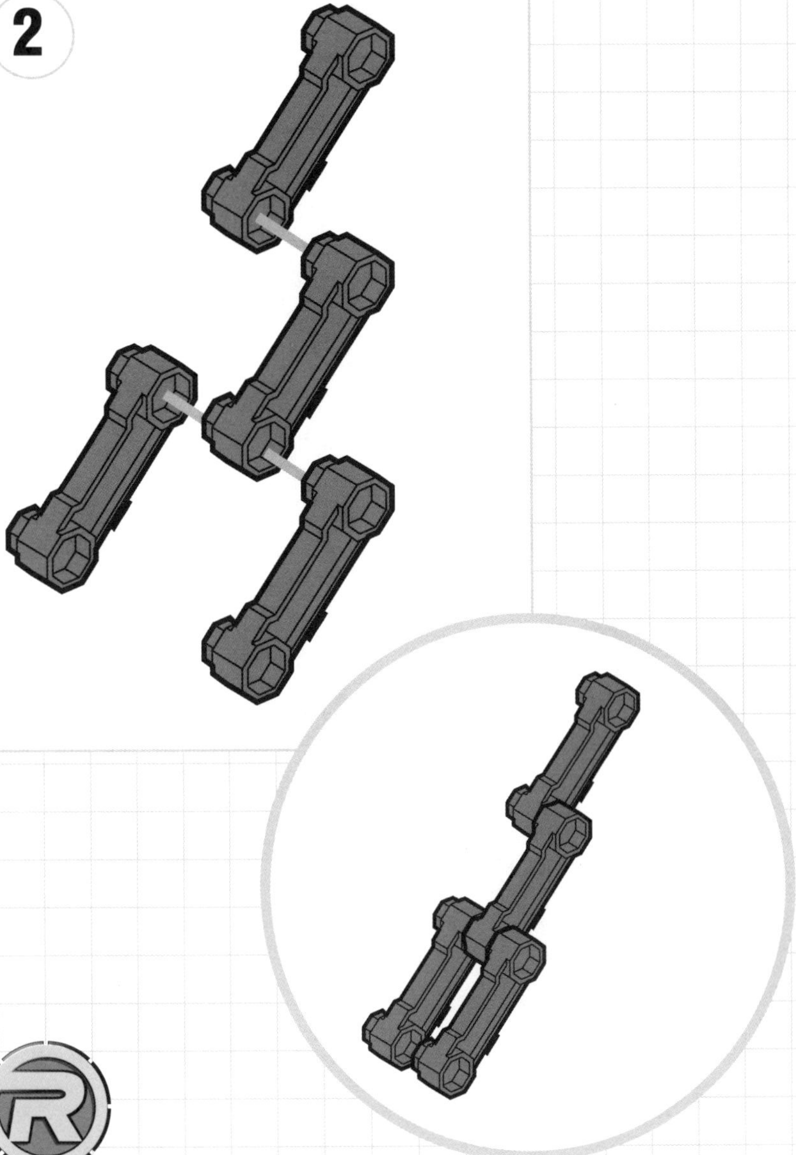

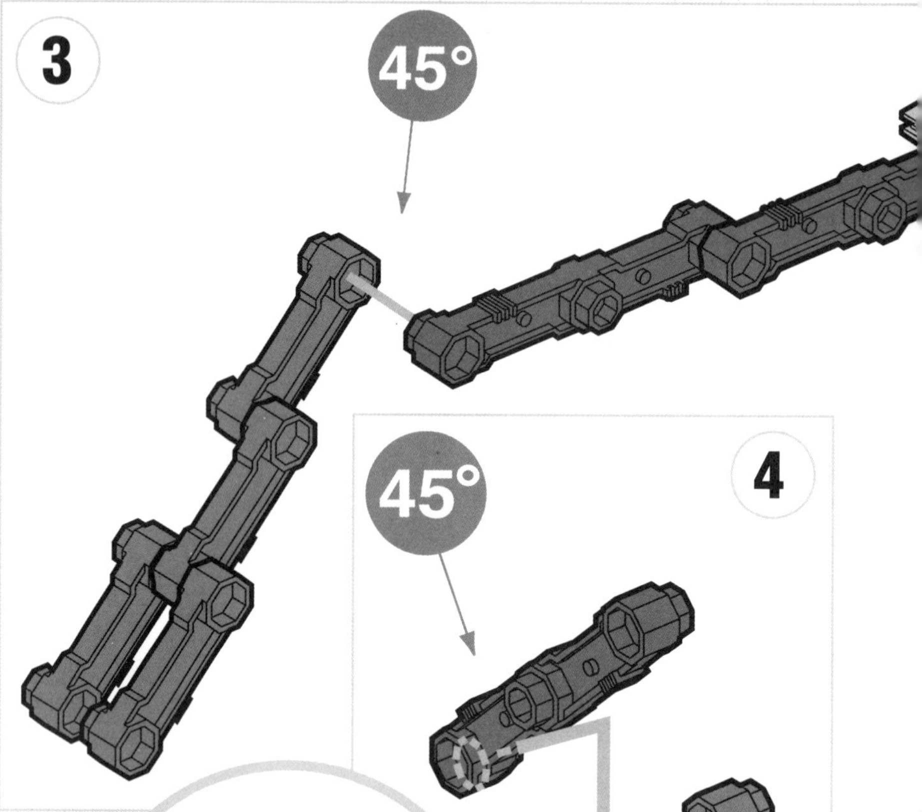
3
45°

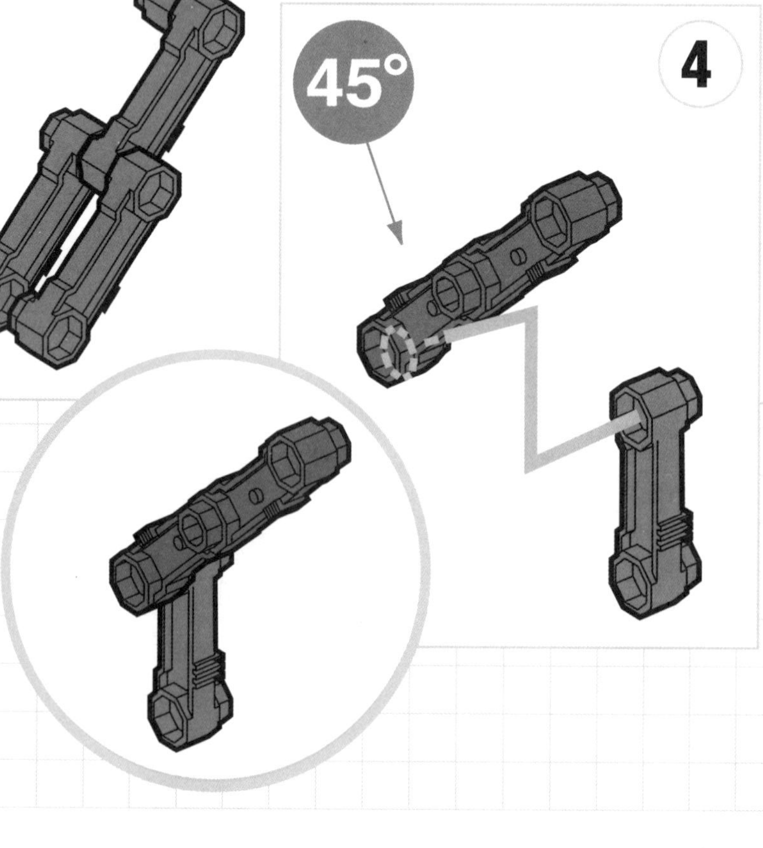
45°
4

5

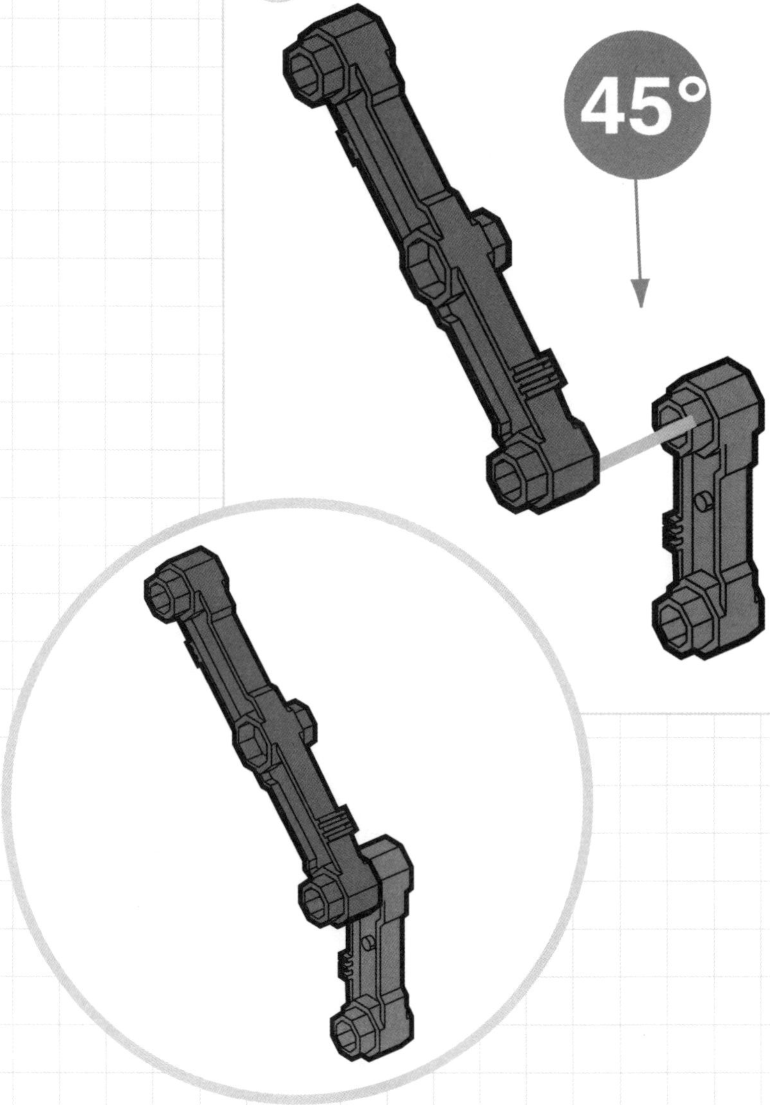

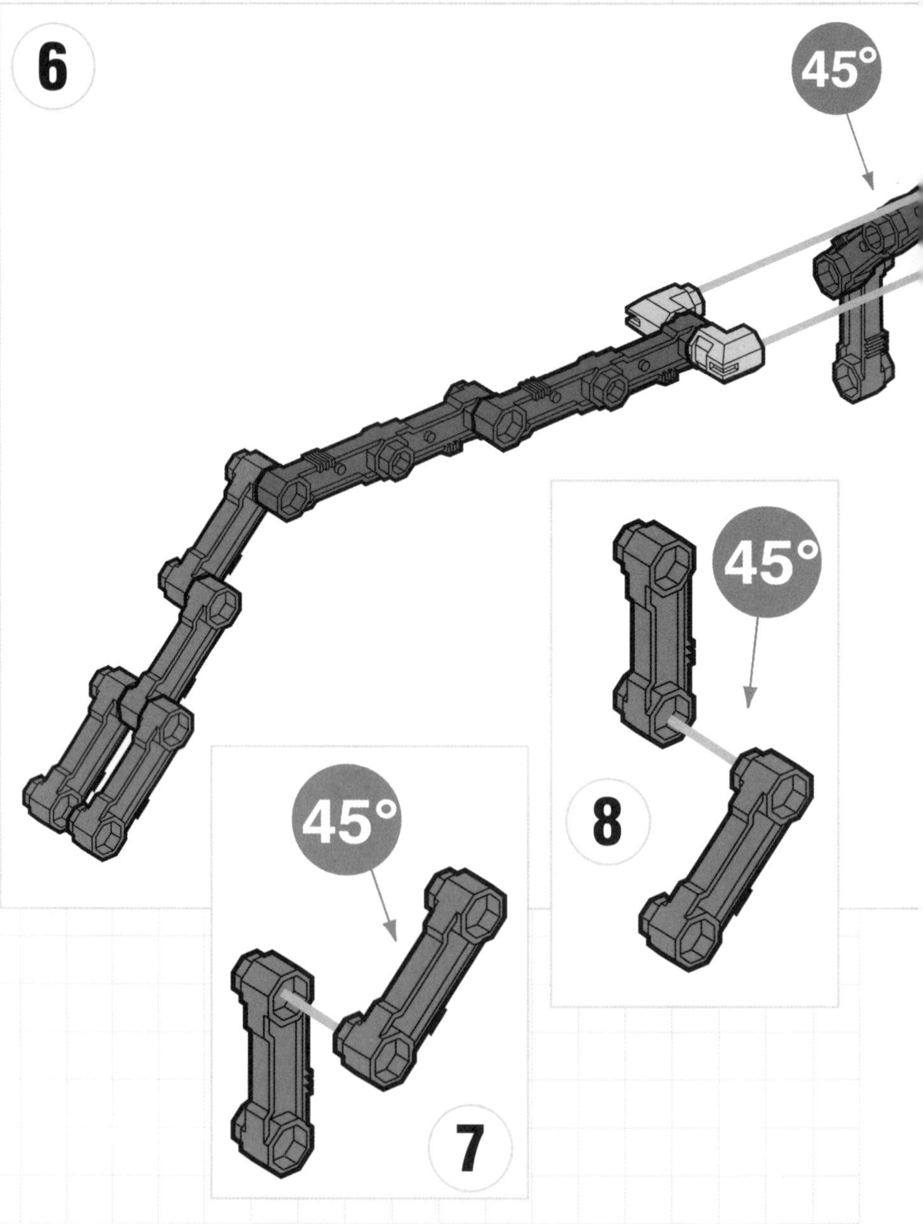
6
45°
45°
8
45°
7

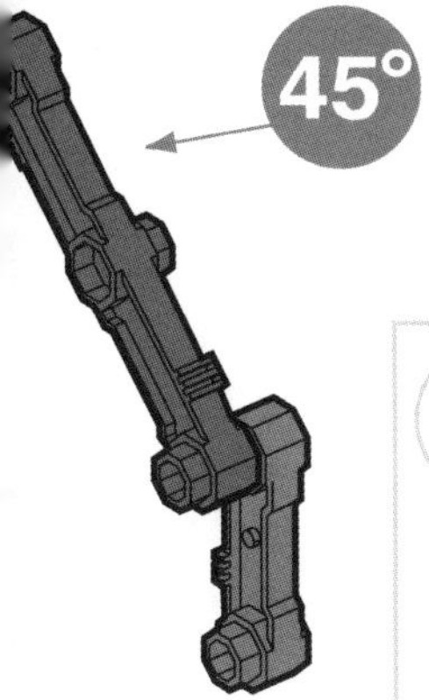
45°

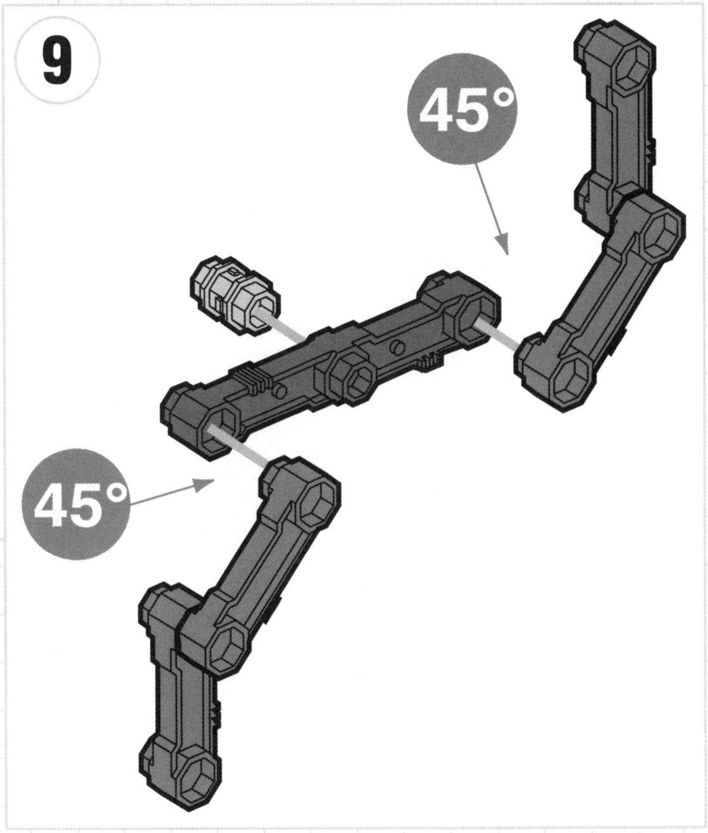
9
45°
45°

10

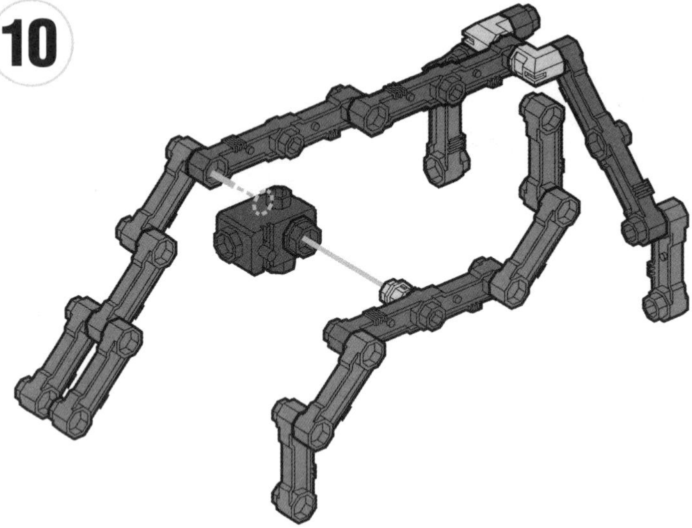

11

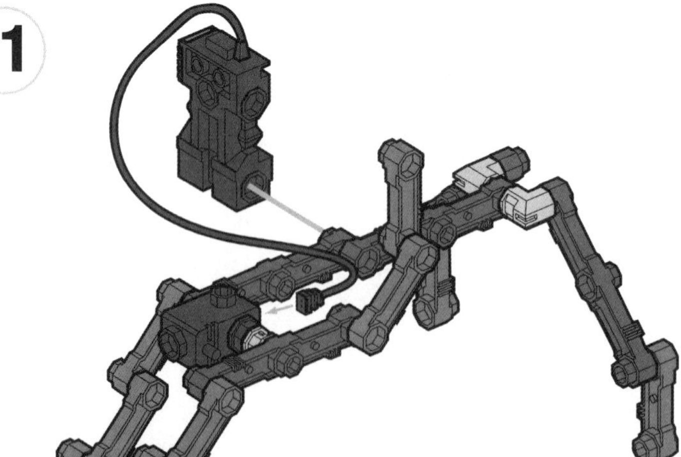

Challenge Five:
The Robot Zoo

Robot inventors have always been intrigued by the idea of "robotic animals." Recent years have seen the introduction of robotic dogs, robotic spiders, even robotic fish! Not only do these robots simulate an animal's movement and behavior, but they sometimes include artificial fur, feathers, and even fish scales!

In this challenge, you need to design a robotic pet to call your own.

What You'll Need:

- **paper or construction paper**
- **scissors**
- **markers**
- **tape**
- **glue (optional)**
- **assorted small objects such as feathers, straws, toothpicks, etc.**

Get started:

First decide what animal you want to create (you might get ideas by drawing a picture). Then decide what part of the animal you would like to move. Will it be a robotic dog with a wagging tail? Or a robot crocodile with a mouth that opens and closes? After you begin to design your animal, you can add additional parts to enhance its appearance. A robotic turkey could have bright paper feathers on its tail. A robotic tyrannasaurus should have large white paper teeth. Let your imagination go wild—and your animals will fly, run, crawl, or slither to the zoo!

Challenge Six:
Robot Inventions

In this challenge, you must design a robot that will perform an everyday task around the house. Maybe your robot will ring the doorbell, pour bubble bath into the tub, turn the pages in a phone book, or spread peanut butter on a slice of bread.

Get started:

To find the perfect job for your robot, just take a walk around your house. Are there any chores that need to be done? Once you've found the perfect task, design a robot that will meet the challenge.

Whatever you design, make sure it has a catchy name—like The BubbleBathBot™ or the DoorBellBot™. If you're ever going to build robots for a living, you'll want to sell them in stores and make lots of money!

And who knows—maybe one day, *you'll* be writing the book on robots!

For More Information

Books:

Asimov, Isaac. ***I Robot.*** New York: Doubleday, 1951.

Cook, J.. ***How To Draw Robots and Aliens.*** EDC Publications. 1993.

Potter, Tony and Guild, Ivor. An Usborne Introduction—***Robotics,*** Revised Ed., EDC Publishing. 1993.

Wickelgren, Ingrid. ***Ramblin' Robots —Building A Breed of Mechanical Beasts,*** Franklin Watts.1996.

Internet Sites:

Robotics Internet Resources Page
This site links to robot web sites around the world.
http://piglet.cs.umass.edu:4321/robotics.html

Space Robotics Site
Visit NASA on this site.
http://robotics.jpl.nasa.gov

Robotix® Home Page
www.robotix.net

Calling All Inventors!

If you invent a fun or exciting robot using this kit, we'd love to see your work. Please send a photograph with your name, age, address, and phone number to:

Jason Rekulak, Director of Robotic Science
Running Press
125 S. 22nd Street
Philadelphia, PA 19106

About the authors

Gregory I. Vogt was born and raised in Milwaukee, Wisconsin. He has been a science teacher and science museum director and now works in education programs at the NASA Johnson Space Center in Houston, Texas

Deborah A. Shearer was born and raised in Houston, Texas. She was an elementary science and social studies teacher for many years and is now an assistant principal in LaPorte, Texas.

Photography credits

Adept Technology, Inc.: p. 15

AP/Wide World Photos: pp. 13, 16, 26 center, 31

Courtesy Canadian Space Agency © 1999, <www.space.gc.ca>: p. 33

Carnegie Science Center Robotics exhibit, Pittsburgh, PA: front of box background art, book cover inset right, p.19

"The Day the Earth Stood Still" © 1951 Twentieth Century Fox Film Corp. All rights reserved. Photograph provided by Everett Collection: book cover background art, p. 5

FANUC Robotics North America, Inc.: pp.12 bottom, 17, 20, 26 bottom

H. Armstrong Roberts:
- Wendell Metzen: p. 8
- Richard Benson: p. 9
- Phil Degginger: p. 25

John Bechtold/International Stock: p. 10

I, Robot book cover photo provided by Special Collections Department, Temple University Library and reproduced by permission of Ballantine Books, a Division of Random House, Inc.: p. 11

Photography by Stephen Mullen: box front, box back, book cover inset bottom, pp. 36, 37

NASA/Bill Ingalls: book cover inset left, p.14

NASA/JPL: p. 1

NASA/Johnson Space Center: p. 27

NASA: pp. 21, 22, 26 top, 28

Gregory Vogt: p. 61